Text copyright © 1984, 2015 by Harriet Ziefert
Illustrations copyright © 2015 by Fred Blunt
All rights reserved
CIP data is available.
Published in the United States 2015 by
🍎 Blue Apple Books
515 Valley Street, Maplewood, NJ 07040
www.blueapplebooks.com

Printed in China
Paperback ISBN: 978-1-60905-460-1
Hardcover ISBN: 978-1-60905-576-9
1 3 5 7 9 10 8 6 4 2
02/15

The BANANA BUNCH

and the
Birthday Party!

Harriet Ziefert

illustrations by Fred Blunt

BLUE 🍎 APPLE

Meet
The BANANA BUNCH

Lucas

Molly

Scruffy

Jack

Sue

Sam

Scott

Chapter One
New Business

Here's a group of friends.

They've named themselves the Banana Bunch.

Right now, they're off to a meeting

at their clubhouse.

You can go with them.

There's plenty of room.

Meet the gang.

There's Lucas, Sam, Jack,

Molly, Sue, Scott, and Scruffy.

Lucas wears glasses.

Sam has freckles.

Jack is tall, and Molly is not.

Sue has braids, and Scott does not.

And Scruffy is Scruffy. He's also Molly's dog.

"Let's start this meeting now," says Lucas.

"Okay," says Sam. "If everyone will be quiet,

I'll give the treasurer's report."

"Shh!" shouts Sue.

Finally Sam announces that the Banana Bunch

has $12.42.

"Wow!" says Jack. "We're rich!"

Then Molly says, "This clubhouse is too small!

I think we should make it bigger."

"Agreed," says Scott.

"But how?" asks Sam.

Molly answers, "We can add a porch."

"I don't think we should bother," says Lucas.

"Building this clubhouse was hard enough!"

"But we can try to make it better," insists Molly.

"I'll send Scruffy to get some rope."

After Scruffy leaves, Sue says,

"I have important new business."

Everyone gets pretty quiet when Sue says

"important."

"You all may have forgotten, but I didn't.

Tomorrow is Scruffy's birthday."

"What can we do for his birthday?"

asks Lucas.

"Why should we do anything?" asks Jack.

"Scruffy is just a dog!"

"He's not just a dog!" says Sue.

"He's a special dog, who also happens

to be a regular member of our club.

I think we should have a party."

"I think we should buy Scruffy a present,"

adds Sam.

"Let's vote," says Lucas.

"Yeses stand up and nos stay down,"

says Molly.

Lucas looks around and counts.

"There are six yeses and zero nos—

the vote is unanimous!"

"I'd like to buy the present," says Sam.

"I'd like to go with him," says Jack.

"Me, too," says Sue.

"And me, too," says Lucas.

"I'll stay with Molly and Scruffy.

We can fix the clubhouse," says Scott.

"Good idea," says Sam.

"If you two stay here with Scruffy,

then the present we buy will be a surprise."

Molly and Scott sit down to wait for Scruffy.

Before long, they hear him.

"Scruffy, Scruffy, we're here!" shouts Scott.

Scruffy heads straight for Molly.

He stops at her feet, then drops the rope.

Molly gives Scruffy a pat and says,

"I knew you'd find it. Now we can get to work."

Chapter Two

More Room

"Let's get moving," says Molly.

"We need to find a couple of broomsticks
to use as stakes."

"Molly, sometimes you're so weird," says Scott.

"Where do you expect us to find
two broomsticks?"

"Follow me," says Molly.

Molly leads Scott toward the street.

Scruffy follows them.

Molly knows tomorrow is clean-up day.

Molly stops in front of a big pile.

Scruffy sniffs.

Scott says, "We're wasting our time.

We'll never find what we need."

Molly is hopeful.

The stuff looks good.

There is an old lamp, a broken wagon,

lots of cartons, some pieces of carpet,

snow tires, newspapers, an air conditioner—

but no broomsticks.

"Come on! There's nothing here," Scott says.

"Just one more minute," says Molly.

Then Scruffy barks. *"Arf! Arf!"*

He sees something!

Molly and Scott run to see what Scruffy found.

Sure enough, it is something good—

a big beach umbrella.

"This is great!" says Molly.

Molly and Scott carry the umbrella
back to the clubhouse.

"Now what are we going to do?" asks Scott.

"Don't worry," answers Molly.

"Just get out of my way! You too, Scruffy."

Scott and Scruffy step aside.

They both watch Molly as she digs the

umbrella into the ground, then opens it.

"That's a pretty small porch," says Scott.

"Well, if you want to make it bigger," says Molly,

"you'll have to help me with the rope."

Scott says, "Okay, I'll help."

Molly doesn't mind Scott's help.

She needs him—and Scruffy, too.

When the porch is finished, they all

step back to take a look.

"Wow!" says Molly.

"Bow-wow!" says Scruffy.

"Meow!" says Scott, giggling.

Chapter Three
To the Store

Lucas, Sam, Jack, and Sue—

all of them run toward the pet store.

Lucas says, "Pete's for Pets will be

a good place to find a present for Scruffy."

"Let's buy Scruffy a new collar," says Jack.

"Too expensive," says Lucas.

"How about a new bowl?" asks Sue.

"Too cheap," answers Jack.

"I know," says Sam.

"Let's buy Scruffy a leather bone."

"I'm sure he'd rather have a real one,"
says Jack.

Then Sam says, "I hope we think of
something super by the time
we get there."

When the group gets to the pet shop,

they still haven't decided on a present.

They look in the window, then go inside.

There are shelves with pet foods,

medicines, and cages.

There are dog collars, leashes, and bones.

At the back of the shop are the pets.

Lucas sees some rabbits. Jack watches a snake.

Sue and Sam pick up some gerbils.

Everyone talks to the parrot.

Someone asks the bird,

"What should we buy Scruffy?"

The parrot quickly answers,

"What should we buy Scruffy?"

And all four of them say,

"Let's buy Scruffy a pet!"

What Should we buy Scruffy?

"Should we buy a rabbit?" asks Lucas.

"Too timid," say the others.

"How about a snake?" asks Jack.

"Too creepy," say the others.

"A gerbil would be okay," says Sue.

"Too small," say the others.

Then Sam says, "Since we can't afford

a parrot, we need to think of something else."

In the corner of the store, Lucas

finds a guinea pig.

Lucas thinks, "A perfect present!"

Lucas calls everyone over.

Everyone agrees.

The guinea pig is just right for Scruffy.

"It's perfect," says Sue.

"Molly will have to take care of Scruffy's pet,"

Sam says.

"Do you think she will mind?"

"I know she won't," says Sue.

"Okay," Jack says, "Let's wrap it up!"

Sam pays for the guinea pig.

Lucas carries the package.

Jack counts the money.

He announces, "We still have almost five dollars."

"So let's buy food and decorations," says Lucas.

At the supermarket, they argue about a cake mix.

Sam and Lucas want chocolate cake.

Jack and Sue want white cake.

"What kind of cake would Scruffy like?"

"Oh, he'll eat anything!" says Sam.

"Even cinnamon swirl!" says Sue.

"Even cinnamon swirl," repeats Sam.

Lucas, Sam, Jack, and Sue head home.

Lucas will keep the present at his house.

Sam will bake the cake.

Sue will be in charge of the decorations.

And everyone will think of something

of their own they can give to Scruffy.

Chapter Four
Party Time

The clubhouse looks great.

Everything is ready.

The gang is waiting for Molly and Scruffy.

"Be quiet," says Lucas, "I think I hear them."

Sue asks, "What should we do

when they get here?"

"Silly question!" says Sam.

"We should all yell, 'SURPRISE!'"

"But Scruffy will be scared," says Sue.

"I disagree," says Sam, "Scruffy's a smart dog.

He'll understand we're having a party for him."

"Shh! They're here."

Scruffy is surprised to see everybody.

At first he barks.

But when he starts to wag his tail,

everyone knows he understands.

Sue gives Scruffy
a party hat.

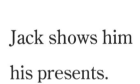

Lucas gives Scruffy
a balloon.

Jack shows him
his presents.

And Sam shows him
the cake.

"Let's eat," says Jack,

who always seems to be the hungriest.

"*Arf! Arf!*" agrees Scruffy.

So Sam cuts the cake.

He cuts pieces for everyone—including Scruffy.

"Since this is Scruffy's special day, it's okay

for him to have a tiny piece," says Molly.

"I never knew cinnamon swirl cake

could taste so good," says Jack.

"How do dogs eat so fast?" asks Sue.

"Scruffy's cake is already gone."

"And he wants more!" says Sam.

"Scruffy, you can't have mine," says Molly.

"The food's gone," says Jack.

"What are we going to do now?"

"I hope we don't have to vote," says Lucas.

"No way," says Scott. "This is a party,

 not a meeting."

"So let's give Scruffy his presents," says Lucas.

"Good idea," says Scott.

"Ditto," says Jack.

"Double ditto," says Molly.

"Triple ditto," says Sue.

"Enough!" says Sam.

Chapter Five
Birthday Presents

"I'm going first," says Molly,

"because Scruffy is my dog."

Molly's present is a song:

Happy Scruffy-day to you

Happy Scruffy-day to you

Happy Scruffy-day

Dear Bow-wow

Happy Scruffy-day to you.

Scruffy thanks Molly with a big lick.

She says, "Scruffy, you give the wettest kisses.

Yuck! Does anybody have a tissue?"

Then Sue asks, "Can I give my present now?"

Sue's present is wrapped in brown paper.

Sue gives Scruffy the package and asks,

"Does your nose know what this is?"

Scruffy answers with a big drool.

Molly looks at Scruffy. "I know you!

Your mouth is watering because you

want your bone right now. But you'll have

to wait until after you open all of your

other presents!"

Scruffy looks at Molly.

"You can wait till later," says Molly.

"And don't whine—it's your birthday!"

Then Scott ties a plaid scarf
around Scruffy's neck.
Scruffy likes the scarf.
It makes him feel important.
"*Arf! Arf!*" he barks.

Lucas's present is in a big box.

Scruffy unties the ribbon,

and Lucas turns the box upside down.

There are old sneakers for Scruffy to chew on.

And a soft pillow for Scruffy to sleep on.

Scruffy sits on the pillow, wagging his tail.

Scruffy watches Sam walk to the other side
of the clubhouse.

He isn't sure what Sam is going to do.

Suddenly Sam throws a yellow tennis ball
into the air.

Scruffy jumps up quickly.

He catches the ball in his mouth

and drops it near his other presents.

Molly says, "It's time for the super-duper
surprise present."

"It's from all of us," shouts Sam.

Scruffy has no idea what's inside the box.

When Jack opens the box,

the guinea pig peeks out.

Scruffy is scared. He growls.

The guinea pig runs back inside the box.

"Don't be scared," says Lucas to Scruffy.

"We bought a friendly pet."

Again, the guinea pig peeks out of its box.

The guinea pig looks at Scruffy.

Scruffy looks at the guinea pig.

It seems as if they will get along.

Then someone loops a ribbon around

the guinea pig's neck.

And Scruffy takes his pet for a walk.

Chapter Six
Game Time

"Do we have time for a softball game?" asks Sam.

"Sure," answers Jack.

"Let's play," shouts Lucas.

Lucas and Sue carry the bases.

And Scruffy carries his guinea pig.

"I want to be captain," says Sam.

"So do I," says Jack.

"Okay," agree the others.

Sam picks first. "I'll take Lucas."

"I'll take Scott," says Jack.

"I want Molly," says Sam.

"I want Scruffy," says Jack, "and I guess
I'll take the guinea pig, too."

Then Sam chooses Sue.

Scott yells, "It's not fair!
You have one more player."

"But you have Scruffy!" answers Molly.

Since Scruffy is the best fielder,
the teams are pretty fair.

Now everything is settled.

Sam's team takes the field. Sue is the pitcher.

Lucas plays first base. Molly plays the infield.

Sam goes to outfield. Scott is up first.

Sue pitches
the first ball.

WHACK!
Scott hits the ball
to the outfield.

Before Sam can get it, Scott is rounding first.

Scott tries to make it to second base,

but Sam comes running in with the ball

and tags him out.

"One out!" shouts Molly.

The rest of the inning is pretty good

for Jack's team.

They score three runs.

After they make three outs,

Jack's team takes the field.

Scott is the pitcher.

Jack plays first base, and

Scruffy plays everywhere else.

The guinea pig walks around in the outfield.

Lucas is first up.

He hits the ball toward third base.

"Hurry, Scruffy," yells Jack, "it's your ball!"

But Lucas is safe on first before

Scruffy can get him out.

Then Sue makes a good hit.

Lucas runs to second.

Sue is safe on first.

Sam is up.

"You'll never hit this one," says Scott.

So he pitches.

Sam sends the ball flying over Scruffy's head.

"HOME RUN!"

Scruffy runs to the bushes to look for the ball.

Everyone waits for him to find it.

But Scruffy comes out of the bushes

without the ball.

"*Arf! Arf! Arf!*" says Scruffy.

"Oh, no!" says Molly.

"Scruffy says the ball is missing!"

Lucas says, "If the ball is lost,

we can't finish the game."

"Well, we win!" says Jack.

"Because you lost the ball."

"No, we win!" says Sam.

"Because we haven't finished our inning."

"Stop arguing!" yells Molly.

"Let's all look for the ball."

Soon everyone hears a familiar bark.

"*Arf! Arf!*"

Scruffy has the ball.

"Three cheers for Scruffy!" shouts Scott.

Molly ties a birthday balloon

to Scruffy's collar.

"So let's play ball," says Sam.

"Wait a minute," says Jack.

"Before we start, everyone should

know they're invited to watch the next

inning of the Banana Bunch softball game."

"Batter up!"

Activities

- Do something nice for someone's birthday.
  Make a card or a present, or bake cupcakes!

- Write or tell a story about "the best birthday ever."
  What made it special?

- Make a list of what Scruffy does that a
  real dog could not. Your list should include
  at least six different behaviors.

Arf Arf

5-15